Lync

WOULD IT HELP TO SAY I'M SORRY, BEETLE BAILEY?

Here's another in the happy series of books based on one of the most famous comic strips in the country. Once again the madcap inmates of Camp Swampy valiantly strive to overcome their own ineptitude—and succeed in delighting us on every page.

Mort Walker again gives us a barrel of laughs in his marvelous cartoons concerning the most unprofessional soldier in the army!

Beetle Bailey Books from Tempo

AT EASE, BEETLE BAILEY
BEETLE BAILEY
BEETLE BAILEY ON PARADE
DON'T MAKE ME LAUGH, BEETLE BAILEY
FALL OUT LAUGHING, BEETLE BAILEY
GIVE US A SMILE, BEETLE BAILEY
I JUST WANT TO TALK TO YOU, BEETLE BAILEY
IS THAT ALL, BEETLE BAILEY?
IS THIS ANOTHER COMPLAINT, BEETLE BAILEY?
I THOUGHT YOU HAD THE COMPASS, BEETLE BAILEY
I'VE GOT YOU ON MY LIST, BEETLE BAILEY
LOOKIN' GOOD, BEETLE BAILEY
OTTO
TAKE A WALK, BEETLE BAILEY
TAKE TEN, BEETLE BAILEY
WE'RE ALL IN THE SAME BOAT, BEETLE BAILEY
WHAT IS IT NOW, BEETLE BAILEY?
WHO'S IN CHARGE HERE, BEETLE BAILEY?
WOULD IT HELP TO SAY I'M SORRY, BEETLE BAILEY?
YOU'RE OUT OF HUP, BEETLE BAILEY

BEETLE, DO YOU CALL THIS A WELL-MADE BED? NO!

6-1

I CALL IT A **POORLY** MADE BED HASTILY DONE IN A SNEAKY ATTEMPT TO "GET BY," BY A BORN CIVILIAN MASQUERADING AS A FIGHTING SOLDIER!!

FOR ONCE HE GOT SOMETHING RIGHT

MORT WALKER

7-3

THE CHAPLAIN JUST COMPLAINED ABOUT THE CLOTHES I WEAR.

8-26

DO YOU THINK THIS DRESS IS TOO MUCH?

HECK, NO

TOO **LITTLE**, YES!

© 1981 King Features Syndicate, Inc. World rights reserved.

MORT WALKER

BEETLE! WHAT IS IT, ORVILLE?

8-31

ORVILLE? MY NAME IS **SARGE** TO YOU, AND DON'T YOU **FORGET** IT!!

HE KEEPS TRYING TO FORGET HIS NAME IS ORVILLE

MORT WALKER